Farmer

Apple Tree
Station

Apple Tree
Village

Church

School

CALGARY PUBLIC LIBRARY
FEBRUARY 2018

Farmyard Tales

Dolly and the Train

Heather Amery

Illustrated by Stephen Cartwright

Adapted by Lara Bryan

Reading consultant: Alison Kelly

Find the duck on every double page.

This story is about Apple Tree Farm,

Sam,   Poppy,

Mrs. Boot, Miss Smith,

a train

and Dolly.

It was an exciting morning at Apple Tree Farm.

We're going on a school picnic.

Mrs. Boot was taking Poppy and Sam to the train station.

"There's your teacher,"
said Mrs. Boot.

A steam train arrived.

"All aboard," said the
train conductor.

"Watch your step!"
said Miss Smith.

The train puffed down
the track.

Suddenly, the train stopped.

"Please get help,"
said Miss Smith.

"The trip is ruined,"
she said.

The children climbed
out of the train.

"Let's go into this field,"
said Sam.

Miss Smith cried, "Stop!
There's a bull."

Poppy laughed.

The children ate
their picnic.

Farmer Dray arrived
with Dolly.

"But we need
a new engine...

...not a horse,"
said Miss Smith.

Farmer Dray knew
what to do.

He tied Dolly to the
back of the train.

The children climbed
on board.

Dolly pulled and pulled.

At last it started
to move.

They reached the station.

"Well done Dolly!"
everyone said.

"I'm sorry our trip was ruined," said Miss Smith.

"Not ruined," said Sam.
"It was an adventure!"

Puzzles

Puzzle 1

Put the five pictures in the right order.

A.

B.

C.

D.

E.

Puzzle 2

Choose the right word for each sentence.

A. "Watch your _____!"

step   dog   bags

B. The children ate their _____.

shoes   hats   picnic

Puzzle 3

Can you count the number of:
yellow sweaters
blue jeans
white pairs of shoes

Puzzle 4

Can you find these things in the picture?

clock   steam hat
train dog flowers

Puzzle 5

Can you spot five differences between these pictures?

Answers to puzzles
Puzzle 1

1B.

2D.

3E.

4A.

5C.

Puzzle 2

A. "Watch your <u>step</u>!"

B. The class ate their <u>picnic</u>.

Puzzle 3

There are <u>three</u> yellow sweaters, <u>seven</u> blue jeans and <u>five</u> pairs of white shoes.

Puzzle 4

steam

hat

clock

train

dog

flowers

Puzzle 5

Designed by Laura Nelson
Digital manipulation by Nick Wakeford

This edition first published in 2017 by Usborne Publishing Ltd.,
Usborne House, 83-85 Saffron Hill, London EC1N 8RT, England.
www.usborne.com Copyright © 2017, 1999 Usborne Publishing Ltd.

All rights reserved. No part of this publication may be reproduced,
stored in a retrieval system or transmitted in any form or by any
means, electronic, mechanical, photocopying, recording or otherwise,
without the prior permission of the publisher. The name Usborne and
the devices ♀ ⊕ are Trade Marks of Usborne Publishing Ltd. UE.

USBORNE FIRST READING
Level Two Farmyard Tales

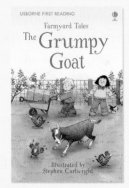

Usborne First Reading
Farmyard Tales
The Grumpy Goat
Illustrated by Stephen Cartwright

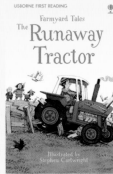

Usborne First Reading
Farmyard Tales
The Runaway Tractor
Illustrated by Stephen Cartwright

Usborne First Reading
Farmyard Tales
The Naughty Sheep
Illustrated by Stephen Cartwright

Usborne First Reading
Farmyard Tales
Tractor in Trouble
Illustrated by Stephen Cartwright

Usborne First Reading
Farmyard Tales
Scarecrow's Secret
Illustrated by Stephen Cartwright

Usborne First Reading
Farmyard Tales
Surprise Visitors
Illustrated by Stephen Cartwright

Usborne First Reading
Farmyard Tales
Pig Gets Lost
Illustrated by Stephen Cartwright

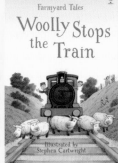

Usborne First Reading
Farmyard Tales
Woolly Stops the Train
Illustrated by Stephen Cartwright

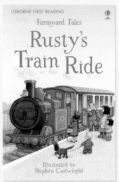

Usborne First Reading
Farmyard Tales
Rusty's Train Ride
Illustrated by Stephen Cartwright